A NOTE TO PARENTS

When your children are ready to "step into reading," giving them the right books is as crucial as giving them the right food to eat. **Step into Reading Books** present exciting stories and information reinforced with lively, colorful illustrations that make learning to read fun, satisfying, and worthwhile. They are priced so that acquiring an entire library of them is affordable. And they are beginning readers with a difference—they're written on five levels.

Early Step into Reading Books are designed for brand-new readers, with large type and only one or two lines of very simple text per page. **Step 1 Books** feature the same easy-to-read type as the Early Step into Reading Books, but with more words per page. **Step 2 Books** are both longer and slightly more difficult, while **Step 3 Books** introduce readers to paragraphs and fully developed plot lines. **Step 4 Books** offer exciting nonfiction for the increasingly independent reader.

The grade levels assigned to the five steps—preschool through kindergarten for the Early Books, preschool through grade 1 for Step 1, grades 1 through 3 for Step 2, grades 2 through 3 for Step 3, and grades 2 through 4 for Step 4—are intended only as guides. Some children move through all five steps very rapidly; others climb the steps over a period of several years. Either way, these books will help your child "step into reading" in style!

For two great dentists:
Barry J. Cunha and Brenda J. Nishimura
—S. K.

Text copyright © 1999 by Stephen Krensky.
Illustrations copyright © 1999 by Hideko Takahashi.
All rights reserved under International and Pan-American Copyright Conventions.
Published in the United States by Random House, Inc., New York, and simultaneously
in Canada by Random House of Canada Limited, Toronto.

Library of Congress Cataloging-in-Publication Data
Krensky, Stephen.
My loose tooth / by Stephen Krensky ; illustrated by Hideko Takahashi.
    p. cm. — (Step into reading. Step 1 book)
SUMMARY: A young child describes in rhyme what it's like to have a loose tooth.
ISBN 0-679-88847-0 (pbk.) — ISBN 0-679-98847-5 (lib. bdg.) [1. Teeth—Fiction.
2. Stories in rhyme.] I. Takahashi, Hideko, ill. II. Title. III. Series.
PZ8.3.K869My 1999 [E]—dc21 97-11829

www.randomhouse.com/kids/

Printed in the United States of America 10 9 8 7 6 5 4 3 2 1

STEP INTO READING is a registered trademark of Random House, Inc.

Step into Reading®

MY LOOSE TOOTH

by Stephen Krensky

illustrated by Hideko Takahashi

A Step 1 Book

Random House New York

4

I brush. I brush.

I'm in a rush.

Oh, no! My tooth!
My tooth is loose!

My other teeth
are still stuck tight.
My other teeth
still like to bite.

My loose tooth moves.

It twists around.

Back and forth
and up and down.

Should I stop
my crunchy crunching?
Should I stick to
mushy munching?

Do lions have
this problem, too?

What do sharks and
hippos do?

I smile.

I frown.

I growl.

I stare.

My tooth stays loose.

It's just not fair.

I want it out!
And then, you'll see,
the tooth fairy
will visit me.

I hop around
on just one foot.

I get tired—
my tooth stays put!

And then one day,
while I'm at lunch…

My tooth ends up
in what I munch!

"Hooray! Hooray!
Hooray!" I shout.
"My tooth! My tooth!
It's finally out!"

There is a hole
in my mouth now.
It will fill up.
Do you know how?

A brand-new tooth
will take its place.
A brand-new part
of my old face!